Jeffrey's Ghost
and the
Ziffel Fair Mystery

Also by David Adler

Jeffrey's Ghost and the Leftover Baseball Team
Jeffrey's Ghost and the Fifth-Grade Dragon

DAVID A. ADLER

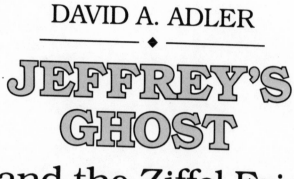

JEFFREY'S GHOST

and the Ziffel Fair
Mystery

Illustrated by
JEAN JENKINS

Henry Holt and Company ✦ New York

Text copyright © 1987 by David A. Adler
Illustrations copyright © 1987 by Jean Jenkins
All rights reserved, including the right to reproduce
this book or portions thereof in any form.
Published by Henry Holt and Company, Inc.,
521 Fifth Avenue, New York, New York 10175.
Distributed in Canada by Fitzhenry & Whiteside Limited,
195 Allstate Parkway, Markham, Ontario L3R 4T8.

Library of Congress Cataloging-in-Publication Data
Adler, David A.
Jeffrey's ghost and the Ziffel Fair mystery.
Summary: Jeffrey, Laura, and their friend Bradford
the ghost attend a local fair where they investigate
some strange goings-on when it comes to winning prizes.
[1. Fairs—Fiction   2. Ghosts—Fiction]   I. Loewer,
Jean Jenkins, ill.   II. Title.
PZ7.A2615Ji   1987   [Fic]   86-14594
ISBN 0-8050-0278-2

First Edition

Designer: Victoria Hartman
Printed in the United States of America
1 3 5 7 9 10 8 6 4 2

ISBN 0-8050-0278-2

To Uncle Ben and Aunt Judy

Jeffrey's Ghost and the Ziffel Fair Mystery

Chapter
· 1 ·

"Step right up, folks. Step right up. Try our games of chance. Enter our pie-eating contest. Lots of fun for everyone. And all the money you spend helps our local charities."

A woman was standing on a small platform at the entrance to the Ziffel Fair. She smiled at Jeffrey Clark, his friend Laura Lane, and the others coming in. She handed each of them a sheet of paper. It was a schedule of events and a map of the fair.

"There's an egg-balancing race soon and then a potato-sack race. I want to see those," Laura said.

"And at three o'clock there's a magic show," someone said. Jeffrey and Laura looked up and saw a short, fat man with a small beard. He was wearing a black cape and a top hat. "It stars me, Amazing Marvin," the man said.

The man reached behind Jeffrey's ear and a

coin appeared. He touched Laura's nose and a few coins seemed to pour out of it.

"Magic," someone else said. "I can do magic." Amazing Marvin's hat floated up, turned over, and landed upside down by his head.

"Hey, how did that happen?" Marvin asked.

"Bradford," Jeffrey said, "stop that!"

The coins Marvin was holding floated up and landed in the upside-down hat.

Jeffrey whispered to Laura, "If we walk away, maybe he'll follow us."

Jeffrey and Laura began to walk away.

Marvin reached for the hat. He took out the coins. "Don't forget to come to my show," he called after Jeffrey and Laura. "It's at three o'clock."

Bradford followed Jeffrey and Laura. But Marvin didn't see him. No one saw Bradford, not even his best friend Jeffrey. That's because Bradford is a ghost.

Bradford lived more than two hundred years ago. When he was ten years old, he was cleaning a barn. A horse kicked Bradford and he died. But not completely. His spirit still lived. And it lived in that barn.

Many years later the barn was torn down and a big yellow house was built. Bradford moved into a room on the second floor of that house. When Jeffrey and his parents moved in, Jeffrey met Bradford.

Jeffrey, Laura, and Bradford walked along the main path of the fair toward the game booths.

"Would you like to buy a raffle ticket?" a thin woman in a red sweater asked. She was carrying a cane and wearing a big blue hat that almost covered her ears. Lots of curly white hair stuck out under the hat.

"No, thank you," Jeffrey told the woman.

"Come on, don't you want to win a prize?" the woman asked. "The money helps the Baker Weber Fund."

Jeffrey looked at her. With the lipstick she was wearing and all that white hair she looked like an older woman. But she sounded like a teenager.

"I'll buy one," Laura said. She gave the woman the money.

The woman wrote Laura's name and a

number on one slip of paper. She wrote the same number on another slip of paper and gave it to Laura. Then she walked quickly away.

"Popcorn, cotton candy, ice cream," someone called out.

"When is the raffle being held?" Jeffrey asked. But the woman was already gone.

"Look at all these games," Bradford said. "We'll have a great time here."

Jeffrey, Laura, and Bradford walked slowly through the crowded fairgrounds. Children were running from one booth to another with their parents chasing after them. There were people selling hot dogs, cold drinks, and balloons.

They saw a woman buy a yellow balloon for her son. "Here, Andy," she said as she handed it to the boy. Then the woman turned to pay for the balloon.

The balloon flew out of the boy's hand. He watched it fly up. Soon it was just a yellow dot in the sky.

"Mommy," the boy cried. "I want another balloon."

Jeffrey, Laura, and Bradford watched a short woman wearing many long bead necklaces throw baseballs at three metal bottles. She was trying to knock them off a small table. She knocked the bottles down. They rolled on the table but they didn't fall off.

"Put out a fire. Win a prize," a girl working in a nearby booth called out.

"Let's try that," Laura said.

"No. I want to wait before I spend my money," Jeffrey said.

A dollar floated out of his pocket. It landed on the counter of the booth.

"Bradford, stop that," Jeffrey said as he reached for the dollar. But before Jeffrey could take it back, the girl in the booth had it. She gave Jeffrey his change and a water gun.

Three candles were burning in the back of the booth. "You get three shots," the girl told Jeffrey. "If you put out a candle you win a prize. If you put out all three you win a grand prize."

Jeffrey looked at the prizes hanging from the roof and side walls of the booth. There were stuffed animals, a clock radio, and a tape recorder.

"Come see this boy put out a fire and win a prize," the girl called out. A few people walked to the booth to watch.

"Come on, Jeffrey," Laura said. "Win the tape recorder."

Jeffrey squeezed the trigger. Water sprayed across the booth and hit one of the stuffed animals. All three candles were still burning.

"You still have two chances left to win," the girl said.

Jeffrey squeezed the trigger again. This time water hit the clock radio.

The girl grabbed a towel from under the counter and dried the clock radio. "Be more careful. Water can ruin a radio," she told Jeffrey.

Jeffrey was about to squeeze the trigger again when Bradford pulled the gun from his hand. It hung in the air. The girl was reaching for the gun when water shot right past her.

"Hey," she said.

"Look," Laura said and pointed. "He put out one of the candles."

The girl turned and saw that one of the fires was out. "How did you do that?" she asked.

"I just squeezed the trigger."

"No you didn't. You weren't even holding the gun. No one was."

Bradford whispered to Jeffrey, "I want the tape recorder."

The girl heard him. "I'm sorry," she said. "You have to put out all three candles to win that. Here's your prize." She reached under the counter and gave Jeffrey a plastic cowboy hat.

Bradford pulled the hat away and said, "It's mine. I put out the candle."

"Who said that?" the girl in the booth asked.

"And look!" she said. "The hat is flying. I'll bet that boy is Amazing Marvin, the magician."

Jeffrey and Laura chased after the hat. Jeffrey grabbed it and put it on his head.

"Will you stop pulling things out of my hands and running off with them?" Jeffrey whispered. "Do you know how strange it looks to see a hat float off?"

"Come one, come all, and watch the great egg-balancing race," someone else called. "It begins right here in just five minutes."

"Why don't we try that?" Laura asked Jeffrey.

"Go on," Bradford said.

"I don't want to race," Jeffrey said. "Let's just watch."

"Watch! Is that all you want to do?" Bradford asked. "You're no fun."

Something was happening to Jeffrey's shoes. They were being untied. As Jeffrey bent down to tie them, Bradford began unbuttoning his shirt. Then his belt became unbuckled.

"Stop it! Just stop it!" Jeffrey said.

"Let him alone," Laura told Bradford. "I'll enter the race."

Chapter

·2·

At the racing grounds a man was sitting behind a small table. On the table were some papers, spoons, a box of eggs, and a small radio with a blue ribbon wrapped around it.

"Can I enter the race?" Laura asked.

"Yes, I have places for two more," the man said.

The man wrote Laura's name on his list. He gave her a pin and a sheet with the number nine printed on it.

"And I want to be in the race, too," Jeffrey told the man.

"Good," Bradford whispered.

The man added Jeffrey's name to the list and gave him a pin and the number ten. He looked at his watch and said, "Don't walk off. The race begins in less than five minutes."

Jeffrey pinned the nine on Laura's back. She pinned the ten on his. While they waited for the

11

race to begin, a man wearing a blue sweater asked them to buy a raffle ticket. The man had a crooked white mustache and carried a cane.

"It's for the Baker Weber Fund," the man said. "We have lots of prizes."

"I already bought one," Laura told him. She took the slip of paper from her pocket and showed it to the man. "When are you picking the winner?"

He didn't answer. He just walked away.

"Gather around, folks. Gather around," the man behind the table called out. "The Ziffel Fair's egg-balancing race is about to begin."

Boys and girls with numbers pinned on their backs crowded around the table.

"This is an easy race to win," the man told the boys and girls. "I'll shoot this toy gun to start the race. Then you run to where those two men are holding the ribbon. The first one to reach the ribbon wins this radio." He pointed to the radio on his table.

Jeffrey and Laura stood behind a white line that was painted on the ground. The others did too.

The man held up his gun. He was about to shoot it to start the race. But he put the gun down.

The man laughed and said, "I forgot to tell you about the eggs." He gave Jeffrey, Laura, and each of the others an egg. "You have to carry an egg with you while you run. Don't let it break."

"That's easy," Jeffrey whispered to Laura.

The man held up the gun again. He was about to shoot it to start the race. But he didn't.

The man laughed again and showed a handful of spoons to the crowd that had gathered to watch. "They have to run while balancing the egg on a spoon."

"That's not so easy," Jeffrey whispered.

Then the man told those in the race, "If the egg falls, you can put it onto the spoon and keep running. If it breaks, you have to come back, get another egg, and start all over again."

The man gave everyone in the race a spoon. Jeffrey, Laura, and the others balanced their eggs on their spoons.

"Don't run," Bradford whispered to Jeffrey and Laura. "Take quick, steady steps. But don't run."

The man held up his gun again.

Bang!

One boy in the race was frightened by the noise. His egg dropped and broke. The man gave him another one.

"Run! Run!" people standing on the side called out.

Jeffrey took a giant step. The egg didn't fall. He took another step. Then he began to walk more quickly and the egg fell onto his shoe and broke.

Jeffrey shook his foot. The egg didn't come off.

"You'll clean your shoe later," Bradford whis-

14

pered. "Hurry and get another egg."

Jeffrey ran back to the table. A girl was ahead of him. The man gave the girl an egg. Then he gave one to Jeffrey.

Before he started to race again, Jeffrey looked to see where Laura was. She was halfway to the finish line. At first Jeffrey thought that she was ahead of everyone. But then he saw a girl with the number two pinned to her back reach the ribbon.

"We have a winner," the man called out.

Jeffrey shook his foot again. The egg still didn't come off. He walked up to Laura and they watched as the winner was given the radio with the blue ribbon wrapped around it. People in the crowd patted her back. The girl held up the radio and waved it. Then she walked off.

Jeffrey took a few leaves and wiped the egg off his shoe.

"How did she do it?" Laura asked. "She was almost running and her egg didn't drop once."

"Maybe she's great at balancing things," Jeffrey said.

"And maybe she cheated," Bradford said.

Chapter

·3·

"I once saw a girl in an egg-balancing race dip her spoon in molasses," Bradford said. "But of course that was a long time ago."

"Where would anyone get molasses now?" Laura asked.

Laura and Jeffrey waited for Bradford to answer. When he didn't, they knew he was gone.

"Where did he go now?" Jeffrey asked.

"I think he's over there," Laura said. She pointed to the bushes near where the two men had been holding the ribbon. "I saw something move."

Jeffrey and Laura ran to the bushes.

"Bradford, are you here?" Jeffrey asked.

"Yes, and look what I found."

A spoon floated out of the bushes. "Look at this," Bradford said. "There's chewing gum on it. That's why the egg didn't fall off. It was stuck to the spoon."

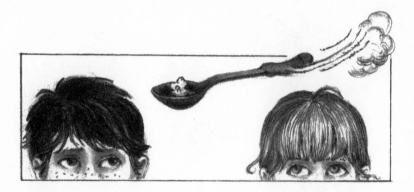

"She cheated. That's not fair," Laura said.

"Don't feel bad," Jeffrey told her, "I didn't win either."

"But I was right behind her," Laura said. "If she hadn't cheated, I would have won."

"The potato-sack race is next," Bradford said. "Maybe you'll win that."

Laura smiled and said, "Let's walk and see the fair."

Jeffrey, Laura, and Bradford walked through the fair, past many of the booths. Then Bradford said, "Look, there's Amazing Marvin."

"Watch this," Marvin said to a small boy and his mother. Marvin showed them he had nothing in his hands. He made a fist. Then he reached into the fist and pulled out a red scarf.

"How did you do that?" the boy's mother asked.

"You'll see more tricks at my magic show. It's

at three o'clock," Marvin said as he walked away.

"I want a balloon," the boy said. "Tell the man I want a balloon."

The woman told her son, "The man only pulls out scarves."

"I want a balloon," the boy cried.

Jeffrey, Laura, and Bradford watched as the woman bought a large green balloon for her son.

"Here, Andy," she said, and gave the balloon to the boy. Then as she turned to pay for it she said, "Don't let go of the string."

But the boy had already let go of the balloon.

He watched it fly up. Then he cried, "Mommy, I want another one."

Jeffrey, Laura, and Bradford walked along the main path of the fair.

"Test your strength," someone called out. "Ring the bell and win a prize."

"We have another winner," someone else called out. "Come and play Ring Toss, the easiest game at the fair."

"Raffle tickets, buy your raffle tickets here."

"Popcorn, cotton candy, ice cream."

"Knock down a Kewpie doll and win a teddy bear."

"Let's go," Bradford said. "It's about time for the potato-sack race."

Jeffrey pointed and said, "The race is over there. It's where we raced with the eggs."

Jeffrey and Laura rushed to the racing grounds. A woman was standing in the middle of a group of children. She was holding up a brown sack.

"I have room for one more," she called out. "Who wants to be in the race?"

Laura held up her hand and yelled, "I do. I do."

The woman gave the sack to Laura. Then she blew a whistle.

A short woman wearing many long bead
necklaces was standing next to Laura. She had
both of her legs in a potato sack. "Hi, I'm
Trude," she said, and shook hands with Laura.
"I hope I win."

When Trude shook Laura's hand, her potato
sack fell. Trude picked it up and said, "I've de-
cided not to go home until I win something."

"The rules are very simple," the woman in
charge of the race said. "Both feet must be in
the sack while you race. You hold the sack up

with your hands. The first to reach the finish line is the winner."

A large, noisy crowd had gathered to watch. The woman blew her whistle again to quiet the crowd.

"The prize for the winner is a one-volume encyclopedia. It was given to us by Barry's Book Store."

"Good luck," a boy holding a sack said to Laura. As he said it Laura heard a clicking sound. The boy looked familiar to Laura, but she couldn't remember where she had seen him. Laura watched as the boy wished good luck to the others in the race.

"Stand behind the white line," the woman said. "Pull up your sacks. Go!"

Chapter

·4·

Laura held up her sack with both hands.

"Jump!" Bradford whispered. "Hold the sack and jump forward."

"Go, go, go," people watching the race yelled.

"Go, Jimmy, go."

"Come on, Trude."

All around Laura, people in the race were falling. As soon as they got up and tried to jump ahead, they fell again.

Laura held up her sack with both hands. She jumped ahead. She jumped again and fell.

"Your jumps are too big," Bradford told her.

Laura stood. She jumped again and fell.

"Take smaller jumps," Bradford told her.

"My jumps are not too big. There's something in here."

Laura reached around in her potato sack. Then she took some things out and held them up. "Look, marbles," she said. She put them in

her pocket. Then Laura held up her sack and jumped forward.

Laura took quick, small jumps.

"Hurry, hurry," Jeffrey yelled.

"Hey," someone in the race said, "there's something in my sack. It's making me fall."

"Me too," someone else called out. He was lying on the ground.

Laura jumped as quickly as she could. But before she had gotten very far she heard a big cheer. Laura looked up and saw that someone had just crossed the finish line.

Trill. Trill.

The woman in charge of the race blew her whistle. "We have a winner," she called out.

A crowd gathered around the winner. The woman pushed through them and said, "I am pleased to present to the winner of the Ziffel Fair potato-sack race this one-volume encyclopedia."

"Don't be upset," Jeffrey told Laura. "You came in second. It's too bad there's no prize for second place."

The others in the race stepped out of their potato sacks. Jeffrey and Laura watched as the people around the winner began to walk away. Then they saw who had won the race. He was holding the prize, a very large book.

"That's the boy who wished me good luck," Laura said. "And when he did, I heard a clicking sound. I'll bet he dropped those marbles into my potato sack."

Laura struggled to get out of her potato sack. "Quick," she said. "We have to stop him before he gets away."

Jeffrey, Laura, and Bradford tried to run to the finish line, but people who had watched the race got in their way. By the time they got there, the boy was gone.

Jeffrey ran to the main path of the fair. "There he is."

"Where?" Bradford asked.

Jeffrey pointed to the Break-a-Balloon booth.

As Jeffrey, Laura, and Bradford rushed down the path, they saw the boy walk behind the booth.

"Excuse me," Jeffrey said. He bumped into a small child holding a big cone of cotton candy. Some of the candy stuck to Jeffrey's shirt.

"Sorry," Laura said as she ran behind the booth. She almost ran into a man who was walking out onto the main path.

"There's no one here," Laura told Jeffrey.

"Maybe he's behind those bushes."

"No," Bradford said. "The boy is gone."

Chapter

·5·

There was a box on the ground. Laura sat on it. "I was cheated again," she said. "I should have won that race."

Jeffrey picked some cotton candy off his shirt. Then he looked at Laura. She held her head in her hands and was looking at the ground.

"It's not that bad," Jeffrey said. "Bradford and I know that you're the real winner."

Jeffrey took off his plastic cowboy hat and held it out to her.

"I am pleased to present this *real* plastic hat to the *real* winner of the potato-sack race."

Jeffrey gave the hat to Laura.

Bradford said, "That boy wished good luck to everyone in the race. I'll bet he put marbles in *everyone's* sacks."

Laura put on the cowboy hat. She turned to where she thought Bradford was standing and said, "Maybe that's why we were all falling."

"Let's go and find out," Bradford said.

Jeffrey and Laura walked together onto the main path. As they walked they passed a man and a woman who were selling raffle tickets.

"We have a winner here," the man in the Ring-Toss booth called out.

"Try the Basketball Shoot. It's easy. It's fun."

Jeffrey and Laura walked past a little boy who cried, "Mommy, I want a balloon."

The woman looked down at her child and told him, "I'm not buying you another balloon, Andy. You just let them go."

"But I like to watch them fly up into the sky," the boy said.

There was no longer a crowd of people at the racing grounds. And the woman who had been in charge of the race was there holding the potato sacks. She was talking to an older man dressed in a suit. He wore a large button on his jacket that said "Hi. I'm Mike Edwards, Director of the Ziffel Fair."

"We can't look through the potato sacks," Jeffrey whispered. "The woman is holding them."

"We can't, but Bradford can," Laura said.

Jeffrey and Laura watched as the potato

sacks moved in the woman's arms. One sack stretched up and popped open. The woman pushed it down and held it more tightly.

"Stop that," Bradford said. "I'm looking for marbles."

"Ahhh!" the woman screamed. She dropped the potato sacks and stepped away from them. Mike Edwards stepped back too.

"It talked," the woman whispered.

"Look," Mike Edwards said. "They're moving."

Mike Edwards and the woman watched as Bradford searched through the sacks. But they didn't see Bradford. They saw one sack after another stand, stretch, and bulge as if something was moving inside it, and then drop to the ground.

"It's almost as if they're alive," Mike Edwards whispered.

"But then they seem to collapse and die," the woman said.

Bradford searched through each of the sacks. He found a great many marbles. He carried them to Jeffrey and Laura. Of course, Mike Edwards and the woman didn't see Bradford carrying the marbles. They saw the marbles floating in the air.

"I'll bet this is one of Marvin's tricks," Mike Edwards whispered. "He's been walking through the fair doing magic. He's trying to get people to come to his show."

The woman looked around. "It can't be Marvin," she said. "He's not here."

The marbles floated past Jeffrey and Laura.

"Follow me," Bradford said.

Jeffrey and Laura followed the marbles. As the marbles floated across the main path of the fair, people stopped and stared.

"How do they do that?" a child asked.

"Amazing."

"They must be using really thin wires to hold them up."

Bradford stopped at a bench and gave the marbles to Jeffrey. Jeffrey put them in his pocket. Then he and Laura sat next to Bradford.

"There were marbles in eight of the sacks," Bradford told them.

"That's right," Laura said. "There were ten of us in the race. I took the marbles out of my sack. That's nine. And I'm sure the boy who won the race didn't put marbles in his own sack. That's eight."

"What do we do now?" Jeffrey asked.

"There's nothing we can do," Bradford said. "Even if we tell the woman, she'll say the race is over. And we really can't prove the boy put marbles in everyone's sacks."

"And we won't be able to find the boy," Jeffrey said. "We chased after him. But he seemed to disappear."

Laura closed her eyes.

"What are you doing?" Jeffrey asked.

"Shhh. I'm thinking."

People were walking past Jeffrey and Laura's bench. Children were crying. Men and women working in the booths were calling out to passersby. Laura put her hands over her ears to keep out the noise.

Bradford pulled one of Laura's hands away

from her ear and asked, "What are you thinking
about?"

"A lot of strange things have happened at this
fair," Laura said. "In two races people cheated
and won. A boy carrying a giant-sized book dis-
appeared. And he looked familiar to me."

Jeffrey said, "And that raffle ticket you

bought is strange. It's just a number on a piece of paper."

"Maybe all the strange things connect," Laura said. "Maybe they're all clues in one big mystery."

Laura covered her ears again. Jeffrey and Bradford watched her. After a short while Laura opened her eyes. She took her hands away from her ears.

"I think I figured it out."

"What?"

"Come with me. If I'm right, we'll find that encyclopedia and the prize from the egg race. We might even find some hats and wigs."

Chapter

·6·

Laura led Jeffrey and Bradford to the area behind the Break-a-Balloon booth. She found a box. It was the one she had sat on before. Laura opened it. Inside were a hat, a white wig, an old red sweater, a one-volume encyclopedia, and a radio. The radio had a blue ribbon wrapped around it.

"There should be a cane here, too," Laura said.

"Here it is."

Jeffrey found the cane on the ground behind the box.

Laura put on the red sweater, the wig, and the hat. She took the cane from Jeffrey and asked, "Who do I look like?"

Bradford said, "You look like a woman."

"You look like the woman who sold you the raffle ticket," Jeffrey said. "But why would

someone put on a disguise to sell raffle tickets?"

"And how did you know all these things would be here?" Bradford asked.

Laura put the cane down and sat on the edge of the box. "The boy who won the potato-sack race looked familiar to me," she said. "We saw the boy run back here. But when we got here, he was gone and I almost ran into a man. It was the man who tried to sell me another raffle ticket. When I sat down to think, I realized that the man was really the boy wearing a disguise."

"So that's why he looked familiar to you," Bradford said. "You had seen him before."

"But why would he put on a disguise to sell raffle tickets?" Jeffrey asked.

"He cheated in the race. Maybe the raffle is a cheat, too. Maybe there are no prizes. Maybe they're not going to have a drawing for the winner," Laura said. "After they've sold lots of tickets, they'll take off their disguises and go home."

"The radio is here, too," Jeffrey said. "That means the girl who won the egg-balancing race is that boy's partner."

"But here's her disguise," Laura said as she took off the hat and wig. "That means she's not selling raffle tickets now. She's probably in some race. And she's probably cheating."

Laura took off the red sweater.

Jeffrey took the fair schedule from his pocket and looked at it. "The pie-eating contest is next."

Jeffrey, Laura, and Bradford ran to the center of the fair. A few teenagers and some adults were sitting around a large table. In the middle of the table were a great many small pies. A large crowd had gathered to watch the contest.

"This is the highlight of the Ziffel Fair," a tall, thin man announced. "The contestant to eat the most pies will win a generous gift certificate from the Crust and Crumb Bakery, the bakery that donated these miniature apple, cherry, and blueberry pies."

Jeffrey pointed to a teenaged girl sitting by the table. "That's her," he whispered to Laura.

"As soon as I blow this whistle," the tall, thin man announced, "you'll have three minutes to eat. And remember to save your pie tins. The one with the most empty pie tins will win."

Jeffrey said to Laura, "And look at the man sitting next to her with the crooked mustache. That's the man who tried to sell you a raffle ticket."

"And he's also the boy who dropped marbles into my potato sack."

Trill.

The tall, thin man blew the whistle. The contest began. Everyone sitting around the table grabbed a pie. One very fat man used both hands to push a pie into his mouth. While he chewed and swallowed, he grabbed another pie.

"Eat, Billy, eat," someone called out.

"Yuch, I hate blueberry," a teenaged boy said as he bit into a pie.

The people sitting around the table were a mess. Their hands and faces were sticky with pie filling. As soon as they finished eating one pie they grabbed another.

"Hey, look," Jeffrey said. He pointed to the

boy wearing the crooked mustache. "After he eats a pie he gives *her* the tin. They're cheating again."

"It's time someone taught those two a lesson," Bradford said.

"What are you going to do?" Jeffrey asked.

Laura pointed. "Look!"

Chapter

·7·

An apple pie floated up and flew into the girl's face. Then two other pies hit her.

"Hey," the girl said. But when she began to speak a cherry pie flew into her mouth.

Trill.

The tall, thin man blew his whistle, but the pies continued to fly at the girl.

Some of the other contestants stopped eating and watched the pies hit the girl's face. One hit her in the chin and gave her a blueberry beard. Another pie floated in a circle over her head. When the girl looked up, the pie fell onto her nose.

The boy wearing the crooked white mustache stood up and said, "What's going on here?"

His mustache flew off into a cherry pie. Now it was a red mustache. Then his wig flew off, right into the girl's mouth.

"Yuch!" she cried, and threw it at the boy.

Trill. Trill.

The tall, thin man blew his whistle. "Eat the pies. Don't throw them."

"Stop this! Stop this foolishness," Mike Edwards, the fair director, called out. He ran to the table. Trude ran after him. Her long bead necklaces jangled as she ran.

"That's the boy who put marbles into my potato sack. I'd like to throw some pies at him myself."

Trude took an apple pie from the table and threw it at the boy. It hit Mike Edwards.

Mike Edwards stamped his foot on the ground and cried out, "Stop this! Just stop it!"

"And that girl cheated in the egg-balancing race," Laura told the people standing near her. "She put chewing gum on her spoon."

"That's not right," a tall, thin woman said. She gave her purse to the man standing next to her. She took a cherry pie from the table and threw it at the girl.

Trill. Trill.

"I love it. I just love it," an old woman said. "When I was young there were always pie fights like this in the movies."

"Here, hold this and this," she told Jeffrey. She handed him her umbrella and purse. Then

she took a blueberry pie from the table and threw it at Jeffrey. It hit him in the face.

"Thank you," she told Jeffrey as she took back her umbrella and purse. "That was fun."

Jeffrey wiped blueberry from his eyes and nose.

The old woman opened her purse and gave Jeffrey a few tissues. "Here, clean yourself," she told him. "You're a mess."

Mike Edwards held out his arms and screamed, "Stop throwing pies!"

A cherry pie hit him on his HI. I'M MIKE ED-WARDS, DIRECTOR OF THE ZIFFEL FAIR button. He moved quickly to avoid being hit by another pie, and he fell to the ground.

Trill. Trill.

44

"Stop throwing pies!" the tall, thin man shouted.

Jeffrey and Laura watched as pies flew in all directions. Then they saw the boy and girl running from the table. Two pies, cherry and blueberry, were following them. Soon everyone who had gathered to watch the contest was watching the pies chase after the boy and girl.

The boy and girl ran around a tree and through a crowd of people and the two pies followed them.

Mike Edwards was beginning to get up. The boy and girl ran into him and fell. The two pies hung in the air, just above them.

"Now, tell us about the egg-balancing race," Bradford said.

"Who said that?" Mike Edwards asked.

"I put chewing gum on my spoon. That's why my egg didn't fall. I cheated," the girl said.

"What about the marbles you put into my potato sack?" Trude asked the boy.

"I cheated too," the boy said.

"And what about this raffle ticket you sold me?" Laura asked.

Mike Edwards looked at the paper Laura was holding. "This isn't a raffle ticket," he said. "It's just a slip of paper with a number on it."

"I have one, too," someone in the crowd called out. "The money is for the Baker Weber Fund."

"Baker Weber Fund?" Mike Edwards said as he stood. "I've never heard of it."

"I'm Betsy Weber," the girl told Mike Edwards. She pointed to the boy sitting on the ground next to her. "He's Alex Baker. We planned to keep the money we made selling raffle tickets."

"Here," Alex Baker said as he reached into his pockets and pulled out slips of paper and some money. "Here are the tickets and the money we collected."

Betsy Weber gave Mike Edwards her tickets and money, too. And the two pies Bradford was holding floated back to the table.

"Of course, I'll notify the police and tell them what you did here," Mike Edwards said. "All the money you collected will go to a real charity. But first we'll take all these tickets and have a raffle. The prizes will be the radio and the one-volume encyclopedia you won by cheating."

Blip. Blip.

The tall, thin man tried to blow his whistle. But it was filled with blueberries.

He gave Mike Edwards an envelope and told

him. "Here's the gift certificate to the Crust and Crumb Bakery. It was meant to be the prize for the pie-eating contest. But I don't know who won."

"We'll raffle that off, too. We'll pick the winners at three o'clock, right before Amazing Marvin's magic show."

Chapter

·8·

Mike Edwards walked with Jeffrey, Laura, Betsy, and Alex to the box behind the Break-a-Balloon booth. Bradford walked with them, too. But no one saw him. They took the radio and the encyclopedia from the box and carried them to the far end of the fair.

Hundreds of people were sitting on benches. Others were sitting on the ground. Amazing Marvin was standing on a platform. The magic show was about to begin.

Mike Edwards led Betsy Weber and Alex Baker onto the platform. Mike Edwards held up his hands.

Soon the crowd was quiet. Mike Edwards put down his hands. "Before Amazing Marvin begins the show, we will pick three raffle winners."

Marvin took off his hat. Mike Edwards and

Alex put the raffle tickets into the hat.

Mike Edwards held up the radio with one hand. With his other hand he reached into the hat, pulled out a raffle ticket, and called out, "And the winner is Bill Stevens."

An old man walked slowly to the platform. Mike Edwards gave him the radio. The man turned the radio on and loud music began to play.

"No. I don't want it," the man said and tried to give the radio back. "It plays that horrible music."

Mike Edwards changed the channel to a station playing softer music.

"That's better. Thank you," the man said as he walked off the platform.

Mike Edwards reached into Marvin's hat and pulled out another raffle ticket and called out, "And the winner of the encyclopedia is Don Harris."

A young man walked to the platform. Mike Edwards gave him the encyclopedia.

Mike Edwards reached into the hat a third time and pulled out a raffle ticket. "And the winner of the gift certificate to the Crust and Crumb Bakery is Trude Evans."

Trude ran to the platform, shouting, "I won! I won!" Her many bead necklaces jingled as she ran.

After Trude walked off the platform Mike Edwards gave Marvin his hat. Then he waved to the audience and said, "Enjoy the magic show."

"They'll enjoy the show," Bradford whispered to Jeffrey and Laura. "Even Marvin will be amazed at some of the magic I help him to do."

Mike Edwards led Betsy Weber and Alex Baker off the platform.

"For my first trick . . ." Marvin said. But before he could describe the trick, his hat floated off his head. "How did that happen?" Marvin

asked as he reached up and pulled his hat down.

The hat floated up again. This time it was too high for Marvin to reach. Marvin watched as his hat floated over the audience and then back onto his head.

The audience applauded.

Marvin smiled and bowed. As soon as he bent forward, his cape flew up and people in the audience cheered.

"That Marvin *is* amazing."

"It's really Bradford who is amazing," Laura whispered to Jeffrey.

"No, it's really you who is amazing," Jeffrey told Laura. "You're the one who caught those raffle cheats."

Laura smiled and bowed. Then her legs were pulled off the ground. *She* was floating. People in the audience turned, looked at Laura, and cheered.

Jeffrey laughed.

And as Marvin watched Laura float he said, "I really am an amazing magician. I really am."

ABOUT THE AUTHOR

David A. Adler is an editor for a New York publishing house and the author of more than fifty books for children, including the popular Cam Jansen series. He lives in Woodmere, New York, with his wife and two sons.

ABOUT THE ILLUSTRATOR

Jean Jenkins is a children's book illustrator who also runs a graphic arts studio with her husband in Cochecton Center, New York. She illustrated the first two books in David Adler's Jeffrey's Ghost series.